CINDERELLIOT

A Scrumptious Fairytale

Written by MARK CEILLEY and
RACHEL SMOKA-RICHARDSON

Illustrated by
STEPHANIE LABERIS

RP KIDS
PHILADELPHIA

Running Press Kids
Hachette Book Group
1290 Avenue of the Americas, New York, NY 10104
www.runningpress.com/rpkids
@RP_Kids

Printed in China

First Edition: May 2022

Published by Running Press Kids, an imprint of Perseus Books, LLC, a subsidiary of Hachette Book
Group, Inc. The Running Press Kids name and logo is a trademark of the Hachette Book Group.

The Hachette Speakers Bureau provides a wide range of authors for speaking events.
To find out more, go to www.hachettespeakersbureau.com or call (866) 376-6591.

The publisher is not responsible for websites (or their content)
that are not owned by the publisher.

Print book cover and interior design by Frances J. Soo Ping Chow.

Library of Congress Cataloging-in-Publication Data
Names: Ceilley, Mark, author. | Smoka-Richardson, Rachel, author. | Laberis, Steph, illustrator.
Title: Cinderelliot / by Mark Ceilley and Rachel Smoka-Richardson ;
illustrated by Stephanie Laberis. Other titles: Cinderella. English.
Description: First edition. | New York, NY : Running Press Kids, 2022. | Audience: Ages 4-8. |
Summary: In this retelling of Cinderella, Cinderelliot enters a royal baking competition,
hoping to win the heart of the prince. Identifiers: LCCN 2021002957 (print) |
LCCN 2021002958 (ebook) | ISBN 9780762499595 (hardcover) | ISBN 9780762499601 (ebook) |
ISBN 9780762499618 (ebook) | ISBN 9780762499700 (ebook) | ISBN 9780762499717 (ebook)
Subjects: CYAC: Gays—Fiction. | Baking—Fiction. | Stepfamilies—Fiction. | Love—Fiction.
Classification: LCC PZ7.1.C46465 Ci 2022 (print) | LCC PZ7.1.C46465 (ebook) |
DDC [E]—dc23LC record available at https://lccn.loc.gov/2021002957LC
ebook record available at https://lccn.loc.gov/2021002958

ISBNs: 978-0-7624-9959-5 (hardcover), 978-0-7624-9970-0 (ebook),
978-0-7624-9960-1 (ebook), 978-0-7624-9971-7 (ebook)

APS

10 9 8 7 6 5 4 3 2 1

For my husband, Mark Bergaas—M. C.

For Dan, and our dogs, Charlotte and Hazel—R. S-R.

For BJ, JP, GD & the one & only fabulous Phil—S. L.

Cinderelliot loved to bake.

Every day he measured and mixed, chopped and kneaded.

He took pride in his pies, cakes, bars, and breads.

But Cinderelliot wished for more.

If only someone could love him as much as they loved his baking.

Instead, he spent his days baking for
his stepsister and stepbrother, who loved to eat.
"Éclairs!" screeched Neville.
"Cannoli!" yelled Gertrude.

With a sigh, Cinderelliot served
delicious creations to his stepsiblings.

One day, a letter arrived.

Hear ye! Hear ye!
Prince Samuel seeks a skilled baker for the palace.
Enter the Royal Baking Competition.
Win a place in the Prince's heart and home.

"Cinderelliot, make me cream puffs
for the competition," said Neville.

"I'll win with your apple strudel," said Gertrude.

So Cinderelliot sliced and sifted,
whisked and rolled.

Meanwhile, Neville and Gertrude spent hours
deciding what to wear.
"I wish I could enter the competition," said Cinderelliot.

"No," said Neville. "You have to wash the dishes."
"You're filthy and covered in batter," said Gertrude.

They scooped up Cinderelliot's desserts
and headed to the palace.

"I wish I could go to the palace and bake for the prince,"
said Cinderelliot, while cleaning up.

Suddenly, a shower of sprinkles filled the kitchen.

"What do we have here?" asked a spectacular man.

Cinderelliot wiped his face. "Who are you?"

"I'm Ludwig, your fairy godfather,
of course. I've come to grant your wish."

Ludwig waved his wand.
Cinderelliot now wore a chef's hat and coat.

"You look marvelous!" said Ludwig. "Now, bake a fabulous cake."
Cinderelliot blended and creamed, folded and whipped.
He popped the cake into the oven.

Ludwig waved his wand.
The kitchen sparkled.

Cinderelliot and his cake were ready for the competition!

"How will I get to the palace?" he asked. "The competition is almost over."

"Oh please! I've thought of everything," said Ludwig. "Take my limo."

"Thank you!" said Cinderelliot.

"You go, girl! You must be home by midnight.
The magic wears off by then."
Ludwig waved his wand one last time and,
in a puff of flour dust, disappeared.

At the palace, Prince Samuel tasted dessert after dessert.
"Have a cream puff!" said Neville.
"Try some strudel!" said Gertrude.

Just then, a towering cake caught Prince Samuel's eye.
"Who made this fine-looking dessert?" he asked.

Cinderelliot peeked around the cake.
"Me," he said.

Their eyes locked.

"Sweet," Prince Samuel said. "Chocolate! My favorite!"
"Mine too," said Cinderelliot.

DONG! DONG! DONG!
"It's midnight!" Cinderelliot gasped.
"Where are you going?" Prince Samuel called out.
"I don't even know your name."
DONG! DONG! DONG!

As Cinderelliot rushed down the steps,
his chef's hat fell off his head.
He sped away in the limo just in time.

The next morning, Cinderelliot made croissants for breakfast
while his stepsiblings complained.

DING! DONG!

Neville opened the door. "Helllloo Prince Samuel!" he said.
"Would you like a croissant that I made?" asked Gertrude.

"I'm looking for the person who belongs with this hat,"
said Prince Samuel.

Neville wriggled. Too big.

Gertrude wrestled. Too small.

"Does anyone else live here?" asked Prince Samuel.

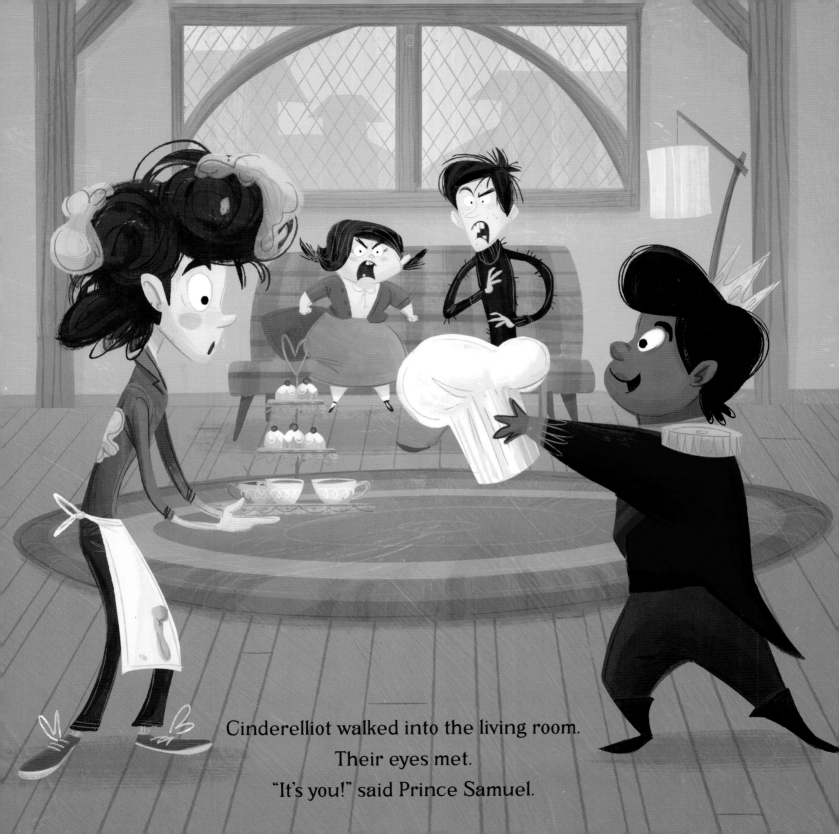

Cinderelliot walked into the living room.
Their eyes met.
"It's you!" said Prince Samuel.

Prince Samuel placed the hat on Cinderelliot.
It fit perfectly.

"You found your baker," Cinderelliot said.

"I found more than just a baker," Prince Samuel said.

Prince Samuel and Cinderelliot hosted the biggest wedding in the kingdom.
Cinderelliot baked the wedding cake, of course.

And they lived scrumptiously ever after.